THE ★
KID FROM
PLANET Z

TO JEFF AND AMY,
WHO OFTEN LOOK AT ME LIKE
I'M FROM OUTER SPACE, BUT
LOVE ME ANYWAY. XOXO
—NK

FOR PIPO—LT

## GROSSET & DUNLAP
Penguin Young Readers Group
An Imprint of Penguin Random House LLC

Text copyright © 2017 by Nancy Krulik. Illustrations copyright
© 2017 by Penguin Random House LLC. All rights reserved.
Published by Grosset & Dunlap, an imprint of Penguin Random House LLC,
345 Hudson Street, New York, New York 10014. GROSSET & DUNLAP
is a trademark of Penguin Random House LLC. Manufactured in China.

*Library of Congress Cataloging-in-Publication Data is available.*

ISBN 9780448490120 (paperback)     10 9 8 7 6 5 4 3 2 1
ISBN 9780448490137 (library binding)     10 9 8 7 6 5 4 3 2 1

# NANCY KRULIK

## THE KID FROM PLANET Z

### CRASH!

ILLUSTRATED BY
**LOUIS THOMAS**

GROSSET & DUNLAP ★ AN IMPRINT OF PENGUIN RANDOM HOUSE

# CRASH!

"Ow! *That hurt!*" Zeke Zander rubbed his head. He straightened his bent antenna.

"Is everyone okay?" Zeke's mom asked.

"I think so," Zeke's dad said. "That was a hard landing."

"What happened?" Zeke asked.

"We lost power," Zeus, the spaceship commander, explained. "We got pulled through space. Then we crashed here."

"Where's *here*?" Zeke asked.

Zeus scratched behind his ear with his sharp claws. "I'm not sure," he purred. "But it's not Planet Z."

"Do you think we can breathe out there?" Zeke's dad wondered.

"Only one way to find out," Zeus said. "You go out and try."

"Why m . . . m . . . me?" Zeke's dad asked the cat. "You're the leader."

"I can't go out there," Zeus said. "What if I get hurt? I'm the smart one. We *need* me."

Zeke frowned. There was no arguing with Zeus when he said things like that. His dad was going to have to be the one to go.

Zeke's dad forced the door of the spaceship open.

Zeke ran his fingers nervously up and down his antenna. He was worried.

"It's fine," Zeke's dad called back finally. "I can breathe."

*Phew!* That meant this planet had oxygen in its air. Just like on Planet Z.

Slowly the rest of the Zander family crawled out of the ship.

Zeke looked down. Something furry and green was growing there. Strange.

Zeke looked up. The sky was lit by a bright full moon. Even stranger.

"What kind of planet has only one moon?" Zeke asked. "Where are the other five?"

Zeus licked his paws. "*Earth* has only one moon." He looked around. "Yep. This looks like the pictures I studied in college. We have landed on Earth."

Zeus was the only Zander who had gone to Intergalactic College. That was why he was in charge.

Just then something cold and wet began to fall.

"What is this?" Zeke's mother asked. She used her arms to shield her head.

Zeus sniffed at the cold wet stuff.

"It's called water," Zeus said. He shook his fur. "I don't like it."

"Let's get back in the spaceship," Zeke's dad said.

Zeus shook his head. "We don't know how badly the ship was damaged when we crashed. It could blow up at any minute. We are safer out here for now."

The water was coming down harder. It felt slippery on Zeke's skin.

"What's that?" Zeke's dad asked. He pointed to a big wooden thing nearby.

"An Earth house," Zeus purred.

A house? Zeke couldn't believe it. It didn't look anything like any house he had ever seen on Planet Z.

FOR RENT

That house wasn't protected by a giant glass meteor shield. What would happen if a space rock hit it?

And that house didn't have a floating garage above its roof, either. Zeke wondered where earthlings parked their spaceships.

"That house could be a good place to stay while we are here," Zeus suggested.

"Won't the earthlings in there mind?" Zeke's mother asked. "Are earthlings good sharers?"

"Not the best," Zeus told her. "But the house looks empty."

"How can you tell?" Zeke's dad asked him.

"That FOR RENT sign," Zeus said,

pointing with his paw. "The owners are looking for someone else to move in."

"Someone like us," Zeke's mom said.

"Exactly," Zeus answered.

"How long do we have to live in that thing?" Zeke asked.

"Until the spaceship is fixed," Zeus told him.

Zeke's mom smiled. "Don't worry," she said. "It will feel like home in no time."

Zeke scratched the spot where the furry green stuff touched his leg.

He wiped cold wet stuff from his nose.

He looked up at the one moon in the sky.

Feel like home? Zeke didn't think so.

# 2

# HOME SWEET HOME

Creeeeeak.

Zeke's mom pushed open the wooden door.

Slowly the Zanders followed Zeus inside.

"Hello?" Zeke's dad called out.

The Zanders waited for someone to answer. No one did.

"The house is empty," Zeke's mom said. "You were right, Zeus."

"I'm always right," Zeus purred.

"Aaaaahhhhh!"
Zeke shouted
suddenly.

"What?" Zeus
asked.

"You were *wrong,*"
Zeke told him. "There *is* an earthling
here. She's crawling on my neck!"

He swatted her to the floor.

Zeke's dad looked down.

"Earthlings have eight legs?" he
asked Zeus.

Zeus shook his head. "That's not
an earthling. That's an Earth *spider.*"

"An Earth *what*?" Zeke asked him.

"Spider," Zeus repeated. "A creature
that makes webs and catches bugs."

Zeke had no idea what webs or

bugs were. He just knew the spider was creepy.

"I'm not sharing my house with that," Zeke said.

"Actually, it's *her* house," Zeke's dad said. "She was here first."

"I think she'll let us stay," Zeke's mom said. "She seems friendly."

The spider wasn't Zeke's idea of a friend.

"This house will do just fine," Zeus said.

Zeke didn't think so. The tables and chairs were covered with a film of dirt. And the tiny panes of glass barely let in any light. Not that one moon gave off much light.

"Make yourselves at home." Zeus stretched out on the cushiony couch. "We are going to be here awhile."

That was a scary thought.

Zeke missed the pretty moons above Planet Z.

And that spider was creepy. It all made Zeke want to disappear.

Which he did. With a wiggle of his right antenna.

"Zeke Zander, you reappear right now," his mom scolded.

Zeke wiggled his left antenna. He reappeared.

"You can't go invisible every time you don't like something," his dad said. "You don't see *us* doing that, do you?"

"Maybe the house will look nicer when the suns come up," Zeke's mom said.

"Sun," Zeus corrected her. "Earth has only one."

"Sun," Zeke's mom repeated. "Either way, we should get some sleep."

"Come on, son," Zeke's dad said. "Find a place to rest your head."

Zeke wasn't so sure he was going to be able to sleep. But he figured he should try anyway. So he flipped over and stood on his head.

"That's a good zeebop," his mom said. "Now shut your eyes."

Zeke did as he was told.

"*All* your eyes," his mom said.

Rats! Zeke had wanted to keep his eye *teeth* open so he could be on the lookout for that spider.

"Yes, Mom." Zeke shut his lips tight. Now he couldn't see a thing.

"Don't worry," his mom said. "Things will look better in the morning."

Zeke figured that was true. They sure couldn't get any worse.

# 3

# EARTH CATS DON'T GO TO SCHOOL

ctually, things could get worse.

"Why do I have to go to Earth school?" Zeke asked Zeus the next morning.

"We have to act like earthlings," Zeus explained. "If we don't, the earthlings will be able to tell that we are not from here."

"So what?" Zeke asked.

"They will capture us and put us in cages," Zeus answered.

"Why would they do that?" Zeke asked.

"To study us," Zeus explained. "They will treat us like we treat obi-dons."

Zeke had once seen obi-dons from Planet O. They were in a cage at the Planet Z zoo. They looked sad.

Zeke didn't blame them. Who would want to live in a cage? Just the thought of it made Zeke want to disappear again.

Zeke didn't want to live in a zoo. But he didn't want to go to an Earth school, either.

"I won't know anyone," Zeke said. "I will be the new zeebop."

"You can't call yourself a zeebop," Zeus reminded Zeke. "You have to pretend to be an earthling."

"Why don't *you* go to school?" Zeke asked Zeus. "You're the one who knows all about Earth."

"Earth cats don't go to school," Zeus explained.

"What *do* Earth cats do?" Zeke asked.

"Not much," Zeus said. "They lie around licking their paws."

"I could do that," Zeke said. He licked his hand.

Zeus shook his head. "You are going to school," he purred.

"What are you going to do while I'm at school?" Zeke asked his family.

"Work on the spaceship," his mom said.

"How fast can you fix it?" Zeke asked.

"I'm not sure," Zeus answered. "It won't be easy to find the right metals."

"Speaking of finding things," Zeke's mom said, "look what I found in the closet. Right next to some pants and sweaters."

"What is that?" Zeke asked.

"A cap," Zeus said. "Earth kids put them on their heads."

"Why?" Zeke asked him.

"To cover their fur," Zeus said.

"If Earth kids wear caps, Zeke will, too." Zeke's mom plopped the cap on his head.

Zeke stared at himself in the piece of glass that hung on the wall.

"I look like a geek," he groaned.

"Lower your antennae," Zeus told him. "Earth kids don't have antennae."

Zeke pulled his antennae into his head. He looked back into the piece of glass.

"The kids are going to call me Zeke the Geek," he moaned.

"As long as they think you're an *Earth* geek," Zeus purred. "That's all that matters."

## 4

# DOG BITE

Aren't you going to eat your hot dog?"

Zeke looked at the kid sitting next to him at the school lunch table. He was pretty sure his name was Eddie.

"Am I going to eat my *what*?" Zeke asked Eddie.

"Your hot dog," Eddie repeated. He pointed at Zeke's lunch tray.

Zeke was confused. The dogs on

Planet Z had fur and tails and fangs.
This hot dog didn't have any of those.

Still, no matter what kind of dog
it was, Zeke wasn't taking a bite of it.
Dogs could bite back.

"I don't blame you for not eating
it," said Amelia, a girl in Zeke's class.
"Cafeteria hot dogs are the worst."

Amelia smiled at Zeke.

So Zeke smiled back at Amelia. He didn't know why he was smiling. He was just trying to act like an Earth kid.

Zeke looked around the cafeteria. He wanted to see what other kinds of things earthlings did.

All around him, kids were eating. And laughing. And running around.

But mostly, they were shouting.

Earth kids sure were loud.

"Aren't you going to at least have a drink?" Amelia asked Zeke.

A drink. That sounded like a good idea. He was kind of thirsty. But there wasn't any cold zoda on the tray.

Hmmm . . . That white liquid stuff in the carton looked like it could be an Earth drink.

Zeke picked up the red-and-white tube on his tray. The tube looked like a ztraw from Planet Z. So Zeke did what he always did with ztraws. He stuck it in his ear.

*Zzlurp!* In one quick gulp, Zeke slurped the whole carton of white stuff into his head.

"Whoa!" Eddie exclaimed. "How did you do that?"

"It must be a magic trick!" Amelia said. "But it sure looked like you drank that milk through your ear."

Zeke was about to say that was exactly what he had done. But before he could, a few of the kids started hitting their hands together.

The hitting made a strange cracking noise. It sounded like it

 might hurt.

"Why are you hitting yourselves?" Zeke asked the kids.

The kids all started laughing. That made Zeke laugh. Although he wasn't sure why.

Eddie patted Zeke on the back and smiled. "You're going to fit in here just fine," Eddie told him.

# 5

# UH-OH! WHERE DID THE SHIP GO?

**M**issing? What do you mean the spaceship is missing?" Zeke shouted at his parents when he got home from school.

He couldn't believe his ears. And not because they were filled with milk. It was because he had just heard terrible news!

"The spaceship was in the yard when we went off to look for metal," his dad explained.

"When we got back, it was gone," his mom added. "But don't worry. Zeus is looking for it. He will figure everything out."

Just then, Zeus leaped in through the window. "Earth is one strange place," he mewed.

Zeke rolled his eyes. *You're telling me*, he thought.

"I tried having a conversation with the cat next door," Zeus continued.

"She walked away. What kind of cat could resist *my* charms?"

Zeke didn't know. He also didn't care.

"What about the *spaceship*?" he asked Zeus.

"Oh, that," Zeus said. He licked his paws slowly. "I found it."

Zeke looked out the window. He didn't see the ship anywhere.

"Where is it?" he asked.

"I said I *found* it," Zeus answered. "I didn't say I got it back."

"Huh?" Zeke asked.

"It was taken by a junkman," Zeus explained. "He thought it was a hunk of junk."

"Junk?" Zeke's dad repeated. "But that's a state-of-the-art spaceship."

"Earthlings don't always know art when they see it," Zeus replied.

"How do we get it back?" Zeke's mom asked.

"We'll have to buy it," Zeus said. "That's what junkmen do. They sell junk."

Zeke reached in his pocket. "I have five zoopers," he said. "Is that enough?"

Zeus shook his head. "We have to use Earth money. Or gold. Gold is worth a lot here."

"Where do we get that?" Zeke asked him.

Zeus licked his paw. "I have to think about it," he mewed. "Right after I take my nap."

"Nap?" Zeke shouted. "How can you sleep at a time like this?"

But Zeus didn't answer. The fearless leader was already snoring.

# 6

# FAIRIES DON'T HAVE TAILS

Class, we are in a library," said Mr. Zimmermoon, Zeke's teacher. "Please be quiet."

It was only Zeke's second day at Earth school. But already he had learned a lot.

Like how to make a paper airplane and throw it across the room.

And how to spit paper through a ztraw and hit someone in the back of the head.

And how to make Earth kids laugh by wiggling your fingers under their armpits.

He just hadn't learned *why* Earth kids liked doing *any* of those things.

Still, Zeus had told Zeke to act like an Earth kid. So he stuck his fingers in Eddie's pits and wiggled them.

"Ha ha ha!" Eddie laughed.

"Zeke! Eddie! Please stop that," Mr. Zimmermoon scolded.

Zeke pulled his fingers out of Eddie's

pits. He smiled at Mr. Zimmermoon.

Zeke liked his teacher. Especially his name. He wondered if Mr. Zimmermoon was secretly a zeebop. Maybe *his* spaceship had been stolen by a junkman, too.

Just then Mrs. Wartimer, the school librarian, sat down on a stool.

"Today is a good time to *read* a fairy tale," she told the class. "Because soon you will be *writing* fairy tales."

"Fairy *tails*?" Zeke asked. "Fairies don't have tails. No one on Planet F has a tail."

"Planet what?" Amelia asked him.

"Planet F," Zeke said. "Where fairies come from."

The kids started laughing.

Zeke didn't understand why. He hadn't said anything funny.

"Save that for your story," Mr. Zimmermoon told Zeke. "It could be a very interesting detail."

Zeke shrugged. He didn't think that was interesting. Everyone knew fairies didn't have tails. Everyone back on Planet Z, anyway.

"This story is one of my favorites,"

Mrs. Wartimer said. "It is called *Rumpelstiltskin*."

Mrs. Wartimer began to read the story. It was kind of boring—until she got to the part about Rumpelstiltskin spinning straw into *gold*.

Now, that was interesting! Zeke sat up tall.

*Plop!* Just then, a paper airplane landed in Zeke's lap.

"Amelia made that," Eddie whispered to Zeke. "She makes the best planes in the class."

Zeke looked at the folded paper. It was pretty simple. He could make a better one.

Zeke ripped a piece of paper out of his notebook. He began to fold it to look like a spaceship.

Zeke knew his paper spaceship would be much better than anything any other kid—even Amelia—could make.

After all, who knew more about flying than a kid from Planet Z!

# 7

# KERPLOP!

figured out how we can buy our ship back!" Zeke shouted as he ran into his house after school.

"You found gold?" his mom asked.

"No," Zeke told her. "I found these."

He held up a big bundle of red-and-white straws from the school cafeteria.

"Ztraws?" his dad wondered.

"They call them *straws* here," Zeke said. "All we have to do is spin them, and they will turn into gold."

"That doesn't make sense," Zeke's mom said.

"I didn't think so, either," Zeke said. "But it's in a book the librarian read today. So it must be true."

"How do you spin a straw?" Zeke's dad wondered.

"I don't know," Zeke admitted. "I wasn't really listening to most of the story. I was too busy flying paper spaceships."

"Why were you doing that?" his father asked.

"The Earth kids were doing it," Zeke said. "And Zeus wanted me to act like an Earth kid."

"That's true," his dad agreed. "Can you show me how to make a paper spaceship?"

"Forget *paper* spaceships," Zeke's mom said. "We have to focus on getting our spaceship back."

Zeke nodded. "I guess we just spin in circles holding the straws," he said. "Then they will turn into gold."

He began spinning around and around.

"It's worth a try," Zeke's dad said. He began spinning.

"Okay," Zeke's mom agreed. She began spinning.

"Whoa!" Zeke shouted. "I'm getting dizzy!"

Spin. Spin. *Bash!*

Zeke slammed into a wall and fell down.

"Me too!" his father said.

Spin. Spin. *Smash!*

Zeke's dad fell into the table. Dishes smashed on the ground.

"I feel sick," Zeke's mom groaned.

Spin. Spin. *Crash!*

She spun into a lamp. The lightbulb crashed onto the floor. It broke into hundreds of tiny pieces.

"WHAT IS GOING ON HERE?!"

Uh-oh.

Zeus was back.

His ears were standing straight up.

His claws had popped out of his paws.

Zeus was mad.

And that was *never* good.

# 8

# TV TIME

Aren't *you* going to help clean up?" Zeke asked Zeus a few minutes later. He swept some more glass into the dustpan. "This is hard work."

"Cats don't clean," Zeus told him. "Not on Planet Z. Not on Earth. Not anywhere. Besides, I didn't make the mess. You did. What were you thinking?"

"We were spinning straws

into gold," Zeke explained. "Like in *Rumpelstiltskin.*"

"But we didn't get any gold," Zeke's dad said.

"All we got was dizzy," his mom added.

"That's not the right kind of straw," Zeus said. "Or the right kind of spinning. The man in the story used a spinning *wheel* to turn *dry grass* into gold."

"Maybe we should try that," Zeke's dad said.

"It doesn't really work," Zeus told him.

"But the book said—" Zeke began.

"The story is just make-believe," Zeus said. "A lot of Earth books are filled with make-believe stories."

"You mean you can't believe everything you read?" Zeke asked him.

"Not on Earth," Zeus said.

Zeke frowned. He had been so sure the straw spinning would work.

"*Now* how are we going to buy back the ship?" Zeke asked.

"Someone is going to have to get a job," Zeus said.

"What's a job?" Zeke's dad wondered.

"And where do you find one?" his mom asked.

"Maybe there's a job buried under that green furry stuff outside," Zeke said.

Zeus looked at them and shook his

head. "A job is something earthlings do
to earn money. You three have to learn
to do things the way earthlings do."

"How are we supposed to do that?"
Zeke's dad asked.

"You have to watch them," Zeus said.
He walked over to a small flat box on
the wall. He pushed a button with
his paw.

"Whoa!" Zeke shouted. "Where did those tiny humans come from?"

"Were they here the whole time?" Zeke's mom asked.

"I didn't know earthlings came that small," Zeke's dad added.

"They don't," Zeus said. "And they're not really here. Those are just moving pictures of earthlings."

"They sure *look* real," Zeke said.

"I want you to study those earthlings," Zeus said, "so you can act like them."

"Hey, there's a teeny tiny Earth cat," Zeke said, pointing at the screen.

"Yes," Zeus said. "It's a commercial for cat food. This is the way Earth cats try to make other cats want to eat their food."

"Why did that earthling just call the cat her pet?" Zeke's mom asked.

"Why is the cat following the earthling all around?" Zeke's dad wondered.

"Maybe here the *earthlings* are the ones in charge," Zeke said.

"No, they're not," Zeus answered angrily.

"But—" Zeke began.

"Watch!" Zeus commanded. "The earthling is putting the cat's food in a bowl."

"So the earthling must be the servant," Zeke's dad pointed out.

"Exactly," Zeus purred. "Because cats are always in charge, no matter what planet they're on."

# THE CHAMP!

Zeke stood outside his school and looked around.

There were no kids on the playground.

The doors were all locked.

*Where is everybody?*

Just then, Eddie, Amelia, and a few other kids rode by. They were pedaling on strange machines with wheels and gears. The kids stopped when they saw Zeke.

"What are you doing at school?"
Eddie asked Zeke.

"I am an Earth kid, like you," Zeke
lied. "All Earth kids go to school."

"Not on Saturdays," Amelia told him.

Zeke was surprised. Zeus hadn't
said anything about there not being
school on Saturdays. It seemed the cat
didn't know everything about Earth,
after all.

"We're going to play hide-and-seek at the playground," Amelia told Zeke. "Do you want to play with us?"

"What's hide-and-seek?" Zeke asked.

The kids all looked surprised.

"You don't know how to play hide-and-seek?" Eddie asked.

"We don't play it on my planet . . . er . . . I mean . . . *where I used to live*," Zeke told him.

"Oh," Eddie said. "Well, it's easy. Everybody hides except one person. That person has to find everyone else and tag them."

That didn't seem hard to Zeke.

"You be the seeker, Zeke," Amelia said. "Cover your eyes and count to twenty. We'll hide."

Zeke put his hands over his eyes. Then he smiled. Now he could see.

Zeke watched through his teeth as the kids scattered.

"One, two, three . . . ," Zeke counted.

Some kids hid behind trees.

"Nine, ten . . . ," Zeke kept counting.

Some kids hid under the slide.

"Fourteen, fifteen . . ."

Some hid behind a big rock.

Zeke knew where they all were.

"Eighteen, nineteen, TWENTY!" Zeke shouted. He ran around, tagging the other kids.

"Wow!" Eddie said a few minutes later. "You found us all so fast. Did you *really* cover your eyes?"

"I did," Zeke promised. It wasn't a lie. It just wasn't the whole truth.

"Now I will be the seeker," Eddie said. "Everybody hide."

Eddie began to count. "One, two, three . . ."

The kids scattered again. Zeke hid behind a big tree.

"Ready or not, here I come!" Eddie shouted when he reached twenty. He began to run.

Eddie tagged two boys hiding

behind the school. He tagged a girl hiding under the slide. He tagged Amelia under the seesaw.

Then he started running toward the big tree.

Zeke wiggled his right antenna. He disappeared. Eddie ran right past him.

Eddie looked all over for Zeke. But he couldn't see him anywhere.

"Zeke, where are you?" Eddie shouted.

But Zeke didn't answer. He was hiding.

Finally Eddie called out, "Zeke, you win! You can come out now."

Zeke wiggled his left antenna. He reappeared.

"Here I am," Zeke said. He walked out from behind the tree.

"I looked there," Eddie said. "But I didn't see you. You must have been hiding really well!"

"You are a hide-and-seek champ," Amelia told Zeke. "The best of all of us."

Zeke smiled. Earth games were easy.

# HAVE I GOT A CAT FOR YOU!

fter playing hide-and-seek, Zeke, Eddie, and Amelia decided to go get something called ice cream at Amelia's Earth house.

Zeke didn't know what ice cream was. But he didn't say that.

Earth kids seemed to like it. He hoped he would, too.

"Out of the way, kids!"

Zeke heard a man shouting just

as he, Eddie, and Amelia turned the corner onto Amelia's street.

"What's going on?" Zeke asked his friends as the man hurried past them.

"I don't know," Amelia said.

"It's looks like they're filming something," Eddie pointed out.

Eddie walked over to a man holding a camera.

"Are you making a movie?" he asked him.

The man with the camera shook his head. "We are making a cat food commercial," he said.

"That's one of those things where the teeny tiny cats try to get other cats to want their food, right?" Zeke asked.

"Yeah." The cameraman gave him

a strange look. "But the cat ran away. Our director is chasing him."   .

"Why did the cat run away?" Zeke asked.

"The neighborhood dogs started chasing him," the man with the camera said.

Zeke did not know how that was possible. On Planet Z, dogs were afraid of cats. But he didn't say that. He knew better than to say *anything* about Planet Z.

"It must be hard to make a cat food commercial without a cat," Zeke said instead.

"You can say that again," the man agreed.

"It must be hard to make a cat

food commercial without a cat," Zeke repeated.

Eddie and Amelia laughed. The cameraman didn't.

Just then, the director walked over.

"We're going to have to stop," he told the cameraman. "The cat is gone."

Suddenly, Zeke got a great idea.

"Do you give the cat gold for making a commercial?" he asked.

The director gave him a funny look.

"We pay the cat's owner," the director

said. "But he's not getting any money now that his cat ran away. We have to hire another cat."

"Being a cat in a commercial is a job?" Zeke asked the director.

"Yes," the director said. "But it isn't easy to find a cat that will do what the director says. Cats have their own ideas about things."

Zeke laughed. *No kidding.*

"Does the job pay a lot of Earth money?" Zeke asked.

"I'll pay anything if I can just get this commercial made," the director told him.

Zeke gave the director a big smile.

"Wait right here!" he said. "Have I got a cat for you!"

# EARTH CATS DO NOT TALK

**M**eow. *Meow.*

Zeus sounded like a *cat.*

A real Earth cat.

At least that was what he sounded like until the hair and makeup people walked away.

"I can't believe you got me into this," Zeus whispered to Zeke once the earthlings were too far away to hear him. "That makeup woman painted my claws *purple!*"

"But we are going to get the money to buy back the spaceship," Zeke reminded him.

"And there is all the cat food you can eat," Zeke's mom added.

"How bad can it be?" Zeke's dad asked. Zeus pulled in his claws.

"I'm just glad no one on Planet Z will see me looking like this," Zeus groaned.

Zeke didn't blame him for feeling that way. The purple claws *were* pretty embarrassing.

Just then, the director walked over. "We are ready for your pet cat now," he told Zeke's dad.

Zeus hissed angrily. His purple-painted claws popped out from his paws. Zeus did not like being called a pet. Not one bit.

The director jumped back, afraid. "Is he going to be okay?" he asked.

"Sure." Zeke petted Zeus on the head. "Zeus is a very good kitty."

Zeus hissed again. He did not like being called a kitty, either.

"Okay, then, let's go," the director said. He sat down in his chair and shouted, "Action!"

Zeke watched as an Earth lady poured some gray goop into a bowl.

Slowly Zeus walked over to the bowl. He took two sniffs of the cat food and . . . *backed far away.*

"Cut!" the director shouted. He turned angrily to Zeke and his parents.

"What's wrong with your cat? Doesn't he like tuna cat food?"

"Sure he does," Zeke said. "Cat food is like *gold* to him."

Zeke reached down and picked Zeus up in his arms. He stroked his fur.

Zeus let out an angry hiss.

But he did not say a word. He couldn't. Earth cats do not talk.

"Let's try it again," the director said. He went back to his chair.

"That stuff is disgusting," Zeus hissed in Zeke's ear. "I can't eat it!"

"If you don't, we will never get the spaceship back," Zeke reminded him. "You will be an Earth cat forever."

Zeus didn't say another word. Zeke put him back down on the ground.

"Action!" the director shouted.

Zeus walked back over to the bowl of gray goop.

He took a big gulp of the slimy stuff.

He forced a smile to his
tiny mouth and looked
at the camera.

"Cut!" the director shouted. "That
was perfect!"

Zeus puffed out his chest proudly.

"Now let's do it again," the director
said. "This time with the liver cat
food."

Zeus looked angrily at Zeke and
his parents. He did not want to eat
liver.

Zeke smiled. "Sure," he told the director. "Zeus *loves* liver."

Zeus hissed and bared his purple-painted claws.

"Action!" the director shouted.

The Earth lady poured some fresh goop in the bowl. This time it was brown.

Zeus sniffed at the air. He wrinkled his nose.

Zeke did not blame him. That liver stuff was really stinky.

But Zeus walked over to the bowl anyway.

He took a big gulp of the stinky liver. He swallowed it down.

And then . . .

BLEEEHHHHHH!

Zeus threw up a great big tuna-and-liver-flavored fur ball.

Just like any Earth cat.

## 12

# I CAN'T BE THE ONLY ONE

t's good to have the ship back," Zeke's mom said that night.

Zeus climbed out from under the dashboard. "I told you I would find a way to get it back," he said.

"It was strange that they gave us paper instead of gold," Zeke's dad said.

"Paper money or gold," Zeus said, "either way, I saved the day!"

Zeke wanted to say that it had all

86

been his idea. But it was never smart to argue with Zeus.

"This will take a long time to fix," Zeke's dad said as they climbed out of the ship.

"Yes," Zeus agreed. "The engines are broken. One wing is snapped off."

"We will have to get used to living here for a while," Zeke's mom said.

Zeke sat down on the furry green stuff in his backyard.

He picked a string of sticky spiderweb from his hair.

And looked up at Earth's one moon.

He wondered if there were other zeebops trapped on Earth.

There had to be.

He couldn't be the only kid from Planet Z.

Could he?